Peter's Railway
The Great Train Robbery

by
Christopher Vine

The watercolour illustrat

Published by
Christopher Vine 2015

Printed by The Amadeus Press
Copyright © 2015 Christopher Vine

ISBN 978-1-9088970-53

Four Mile House · To Oaksted · Nature Reserve · Gorse Hill · Oa...

The Peter's Railway Series

Peter and Grandpa's little steam railway originally ran across the farm between their houses and the village of Yockletts. But recently, (Peter's Railway Hits the Jackpot, Book 5), they have extended the railway, by five miles, to Oaksted village.

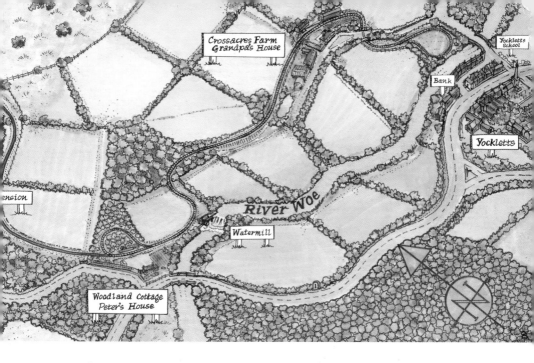

The new line includes a bridge over the River Wye and a long and curving tunnel under Gorse Hill, not far from Peter's house.

This story is an adventure set on their miniature railway. I hope you enjoy following the action on the map above.

The Great Train Robbery

The new Oaksted line had opened last summer and, with the TV coverage, Peter's Railway was rapidly becoming famous!

In fact, it had become so well known that people were always asking if they could come and visit. Eventually, Peter suggested they should hold an Open Day so everyone could enjoy a trip on their line.

The event was a great success and the trains ran non-stop, but the highlight of the afternoon was the naming ceremony for the new electric train. (In all the excitement of their previous adventure, they had completely forgotten to give it a name!)

Over the last few weeks, Kitty had been busy in Grandpa's workshop, making some smart nameplates to fix on the sides. As they were unveiled, the polished brass letters shone in the sun: *Faraday* - the great physicist who discovered electromagnetic induction.

Most of the visitors had been very pleasant and interested in the railway. However, Peter, Harry and Kitty had all noticed that there were four men who did not seem to fit in. They appeared to be curious about everything, but in a furtive, secretive way.

"I didn't like them," said Kitty. "There was definitely something wrong about them."

"I agree," nodded Harry. "They were certainly up to no good. They were asking all sorts of questions about how to drive the train and were constantly whispering to each other."

"They asked me where it was kept at night," added Peter gravely. "I didn't tell them that we just left it in the open tunnel!"

Grandpa agreed too. "We really must start to think about security," he said thoughtfully. "Perhaps I should make some doors for the ends of the tunnel, to make it into a locked train shed."

Next week, Grandpa set to work and made a pair of steel doors, one for each end of the tunnel. They were seriously strong.

Each had a bolt, which slid into a metal door-frame to hold it shut. Then there was a padlock to stop anyone from breaking in.

'These doors look indestructible,' thought Peter, shutting one of them with a clang. 'But if someone smashed the padlock, we wouldn't know anything about it until the next day.'

'I'm going to try to make a burglar alarm,' he decided, 'to add some more protection to the tunnel. It will help to keep *Faraday* safe.'

Peter began work on his alarm by fixing an electric switch to each of the tunnel doors. Then he connected them with a long piece of wire which ran beside the line, across the garden, up the house wall and in through his bedroom window.

The alarm circuit would first need to detect that a tunnel door had been opened. Then it would need to wake Peter up, to alert him to an intruder.

He was rummaging through some boxes of old electrical stuff which he had rescued from the bin. "Ah ha!" he exclaimed. "Just what I need: an old front door bell."

More rummaging... "Even better - a broken torch which has a flashing lamp in it."

Searching in a different box now... some wires, a wire connector block and, finally, an old mains adapter (transformer) from a long gone computer... "Bingo!" he smiled. "The last vital part."

Peter set to work, mounting them on a piece of wood and wiring them together. It took a long time, but at last he was ready to test it.

With the adapter plugged in, he switched it on.

Nothing happened. The bell didn't ring and the light didn't flash. But that was just as it should be - the tunnel doors were locked shut!

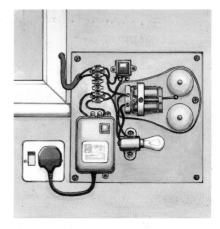

"Kitty, Harry," Peter called out to them in the garden. "Can you help me test the burglar alarm?"

The younger children set off to the tunnel, with the keys to the locks, and opened and shut the doors.

In Peter's room, the bell rang and the light flashed. They would certainly wake him up if someone broke into the tunnel at night.

Kitty and Harry both wanted to know how the alarm worked, so Peter explained it with diagrams...

Peter's Burglar Alarm for the Tunnel

(You do not need to read these two pages to enjoy the story.)

The diagram below shows how Peter's burglar alarm works. There are electric switches on the tunnel doors, an alarm bell and lamp. The doors are shut, the alarm is not sounding.

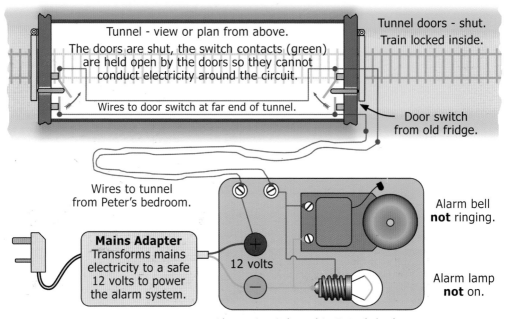

Tunnel - view or plan from above.
The doors are shut, the switch contacts (green) are held open by the doors so they cannot conduct electricity around the circuit.

Wires to door switch at far end of tunnel.

Tunnel doors - shut.
Train locked inside.

Door switch from old fridge.

Wires to tunnel from Peter's bedroom.

Mains Adapter
Transforms mains electricity to a safe 12 volts to power the alarm system.

12 volts

Alarm bell **not** ringing.

Alarm lamp **not** on.

Alarm circuit board in Peter's bedroom.

The tunnel doors are shut and are holding open the contacts on the door switches.
Electricity cannot flow round the circuit, so the bell and lamp do not operate.

Peter stays asleep!

Alarm Ringing!

Someone has opened a door at the tunnel. As the door opens, its switch contacts spring together and allow electricity to flow round the tunnel circuit.
Electricity now flows though the bell and lamp circuit.

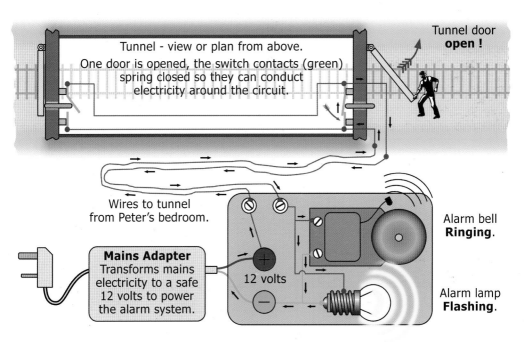

Tunnel - view or plan from above.

One door is opened, the switch contacts (green) spring closed so they can conduct electricity around the circuit.

Tunnel door **open !**

Wires to tunnel from Peter's bedroom.

Alarm bell **Ringing**.

Mains Adapter
Transforms mains electricity to a safe 12 volts to power the alarm system.

12 volts

Alarm lamp **Flashing**.

See if you can follow the electricity around the circuit with the black arrows.
It does not matter which of the tunnel doors is opened, either switch can conduct electricity round the circuit to ring the bell and light the lamp.

Peter wakes up!

One night, a few weeks later, while Peter was fast asleep in bed, he was suddenly woken up by the alarm bell ringing and the light flashing on the wall.

Switching the bell off, he rushed to find the twins. "Quick, wake up!" he whispered. "Someone has broken into the tunnel!"

Looking out of Peter's bedroom window, it was a clear, moonlit night. Everything seemed calm and normal - except for the flashing light on the alarm.

"Look!" pointed Harry. "There's a light moving through the trees in the orchard."

"It's the train," whispered Kitty. "It's coming up the line. Someone's stealing it!"

As they watched, the electric train rolled silently through the garden. On board were four sinister looking men, their faces hidden by black balaclavas.

The children crept downstairs to phone Grandpa.

"Grandpa," said Peter urgently. "Some men have stolen the train, they're heading in your direction..."

"They have just shot past here!" Grandpa interrupted him, astonished. "Whatever mischief can they be up to? The cheeky monsters!"

They were talking for a few minutes, trying to work out what to do, when the silence of the night was shattered by a tremendous wailing, screaming noise. The sound of the alarm was coming across the fields from the direction of Yockletts village.

"I think they might be robbing the bank!" Grandpa shouted down the phone. "They must be using our train as a get-away vehicle! I'll telephone the police. You stay there!"

Peter, Harry and Kitty exchanged glances; they weren't going to miss an adventure like this. Pulling on coats and grabbing torches, they tiptoed out of the house and set off up the line, towards the tunnel.

Arriving at the entrance, they found exactly what they had suspected. The door was open and the padlock lay broken on the ground.

"The robbers have cut it off with bolt-croppers," said Peter, studying it carefully. "But look, they haven't damaged the bolt, it still slides easily."

"What do you think their plan is?" asked Harry. "If they're using our train as a get-away vehicle, then how far are they going to go with it?"

Kitty worked it out. "They're going to come back on the train, drive through the tunnel, and transfer to a van somewhere. Then they'll vanish into the night."

"You're right," agreed Peter. "At Four Mile House, the line runs close to the road. They'll have a van waiting there. What are we going to do?"

"I've got a plan to catch them," announced Harry. "But we'll have to be quick!"

"I think we could trap them in the tunnel when they return," Harry told them with a grin.

"Wow!" laughed Peter. "That would be brave and brilliant. I expect they've broken the padlock on the door at the other end, but let's hope the bolt still works. We can lock them in!"

"I'll guard this end of the tunnel," offered Harry. "Why don't you two check the door at the far end."

Peter and Kitty sprinted over the top of Gorse Hill, to the other end of the tunnel. There wasn't a moment to lose!

They found the other door wide open but, again, it was only the padlock which was broken.

Shutting the door quietly, they slid home the bolt and checked it was secure.

Back they ran, over Gorse Hill, to tell Harry.

"We've locked it," whispered Peter. "The trap is set. Now we just have to lie in wait."

"We had better hide so they don't see us," he added. "They'll probably have the headlights on."

Kitty was nervous. "Do you think they'll notice the far end door is shut?" she asked. "Then they would stop and find us!"

"No, they couldn't possibly see it," Peter reassured her. "The tunnel is on a curve so you can't see from one end to the other. We'll have this end locked before they even see the far door."

They waited patiently, Harry hiding behind the open door, Kitty and Peter peeping over the top of the brickwork.

It was a cold night but they didn't notice.

"How strong do you think Grandpa's doors are?" asked Peter with a grin.

The three children waited in silence, straining their eyes and ears for the approaching train.

"I think I can hear it," whispered Kitty.

"Look! There are lights flickering in Bluebell Wood," pointed Harry.

"Hold still now!" warned Peter, as Harry edged even further out of sight behind the door.

The sound of the train grew louder as it swept round the bend, speeding towards them. The crooks were driving flat-out and grinning. What a fantastic get-away vehicle.

The train roared into the tunnel.

Harry slammed the door shut and bolted it.

Seconds later there was a terrific booming, crunching sort of bang, quickly followed by shouts of pain and rage from the robbers!

Would the door at the other end hold firm?

Running as fast as they could, the children arrived in record time. The scene they found at the other end of the tunnel was spectacular!

The door had been bent outwards by the sheer force of the impact. There was a bulge in the shape of the front of the train, and a slightly smaller dent where the driver's head had hit the metal sheet!

There was a lot of moaning and shouting too.

"Is there anybody out there?" demanded one of the robbers angrily. "Who's there?"

"Never mind about that," said Peter in his most grown-up voice. "We know what you've been doing and we've got you locked up - where you belong."

"Help! I've hurt my head," moaned another voice.

"Oh dear!" said all three children. "What a pity!"

"Don't worry," added Kitty. "The police will be here soon. I expect they'll take you to hospital."

It was dark inside the tunnel and the robbers were angry and scared.

"Now listen here, kids," snarled the gang leader from behind the door. "We've got guns and we're not afraid to use them."

"Let us out, and you can have half of the money!"

Peter stepped quickly away from the door.

"You've got to be joking!" laughed Harry. "How are you going to shoot us from inside a locked tunnel?"

"And we don't want any money," added Peter. "It belongs to someone else."

There was a deafening bang and another dent appeared in the metal door. A bullet ricocheted harmlessly back into the tunnel.

"Kitty," asked Peter. "Can you run to Grandpa's house and get help? They can't get out, but it's time for the police. Harry and I will keep guard here."

Ten minutes later, Kitty was at Grandpa's front door. "The robbers..." she panted, "we've caught them... we've got them locked up... They're..."

Just then, with sirens and flashing lights, the police arrived and leapt out of their car. "Now then Sir and Madame," one of them instructed. "You get back inside. This is a job for the police!"

"But we've got the robbers all locked up," Kitty tried to tell them. "They stole our train to get away."

"They're in the tunnel," she explained. "We shut the doors when they were going through it..."

"Listen Miss," said the policeman sternly. "This is no time for playing games and making up stories. Bank robbers are dangerous. Now, get back inside!"

Grandpa pulled himself up to his full height. "I can assure you," he stated, "that if she *says* they have the robbers locked up - then they *are* locked up!"

"Very well then, Miss," said the policeman, politely now. "Why don't you tell us what happened and then we can take over and arrest them properly."

They listened incredulously, while Kitty told them everything, as quickly as she could. She knew that Peter and Harry could still be in danger.

"Back in the car lads!" barked the policeman. "Quick. Drive to the tunnel. And call the helicopter!"

"I am afraid there isn't a road to the tunnel," Grandpa explained. "It's in the middle of a field."

"The quickest way there is by train. Follow me!"

Behind the house, Grandpa flung open the doors to the engine shed. Quicksilver, the little electric locomotive, was already coupled to some wagons.

"Jump on!" Grandpa ordered the astonished policemen. "Kitty, you drive!"

In a few minutes, they pulled up at the tunnel. "We'll have to walk from here," explained Kitty, "the robbers are at the other end."

Running over the hill, they arrived at the same time as the helicopter. It hovered a metre or two above the ground while armed police jumped out and took up position at the door.

The helicopter, hovering higher now, lit up the scene with a searchlight. The noise from the roaring of the blades and the screaming of its gas-turbine engine was indescribable.

One of the policemen held up a megaphone. "We are armed police," he shouted above the din. "When we open the door, come out with your hands up. We won't hesitate to shoot!"

The searchlight lit up the tunnel entrance as bright as day, while the children watched from the safety of the shadows.

A burly policeman slid back the bolt, then opened the door slowly, always keeping behind it for protection from the robbers and their guns.

The police marksmen kept their rifles trained on the dark entrance - motionless.

Peter, Harry and Kitty held their breath and waited silently, peering round from behind a tree.

Eventually, the men started to emerge from the gloomy hole, with their hands up.

What a state they were in. They all had blood on their faces and the driver had a broken nose.

They blinked and tried to shield their eyes from the glare of the searchlight.

"Lie flat on the ground! Face down!" they were ordered.

"You're nicked!" added the Chief Inspector, as he handcuffed the lot of them.

The robbers were frogmarched back over the hill to Woodland Cottage, where a high-security police van was already waiting for them.

Peter's Mum and Dad were standing outside, having been woken by the sirens, blue flashing lights and now, the deafening roar of a helicopter overhead.

"What on earth is going on?" Mum demanded, as four handcuffed robbers and eight policemen, (four of them with guns), were led up the track by their children.

While the robbers were being bundled into the van, Grandpa tried to explain everything to them.

"But Peter, why didn't you wake us up?" asked Dad, still trying to take in the situation.

"Your children, Sir," said the Chief Inspector, stepping in helpfully, "have been very brave, clever and resourceful."

"If it wasn't for their quick thinking and courage," he added, "that gang would have got away with the entire contents of the bank vault."

"Now," he turned to his men, "we've just got to go back up the line, and recover the stolen goods."

"Peter, could we borrow your train again?" he asked with a smile. "It would be the quickest way to transport everything back to the bank."

At the tunnel, Kitty put Quicksilver and the wagons into the siding, while the others pulled the damaged 'get-away' train out backwards. Poor *Faraday* was going to need major repairs.

What a haul! There were five sacks of money and thirty six beautiful gold bars, glinting in the moonlight. All were transferred to the little train.

Kitty had the thrill of driving it back to Yockletts village, with an armed policeman acting as guard!

Two days later, a ceremony was held, to thank the children for their bravery and quick thinking.

"The thieves took over three million pounds in cash," announced the Chairman of the bank. "And the stack of gold bullion which was stored in our vault."

"As a result of your actions," he told the children, "the bank would like to offer you a reward. So I would be most highly honoured to hand these over to you: Three gold bars, one for each of you. Thank you!"

They were so heavy, Kitty could hardly hold hers.

"Peter, would you like to open an account, and keep it at the bank?" the Chairman asked kindly.

"No thank you!" grinned Peter cheekily. "I don't think it's very safe! I'll keep it in my bedroom and people will think it's just a piece of old brass. Or a box of those Swiss chocolates in a gold coloured box!"

The End.

Why Peter's Railway?

Since a very small boy, Chris has always loved everything mechanical, especially steam engines. The first workshop was in his bedroom where he made an electric go-kart when only 8, followed by a mini-bike powered by the engine from a petrol lawn mower.

He spent many holidays on a friend's farm where there was a miniature railway across a field and so started a love of making model steam locomotives. The latest is Bongo, 8 feet long and the inspiration for Fiery Fox in the books.

Chris wanted to share his love and knowledge of railways and engineering: Peter's Railway is the result.

Books for children who love trains and engineering

Story

Technical

History

Adventure

The hardback books

The five hardback books tell the charming story of Peter and his Grandpa building and running their steam railway across the farm.   At the ends of chapters are special how-it-works pages with simple (but accurate) explanations of what has been happening in the story. In addition, Grandpa tells some wonderful stories from the old days on the railways.   Age range 6 - 12 years approx.

A new steam railway is born.

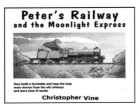

Points, turntables and Peter drives Fiery Fox.

The line is extended and The Great Railway Race.

They build a watermill to power the farm.

Peter helps save the world and makes lots of money!

Activity book with puzzles and colouring. Paperback.

Hardback, 96 pages 17 x 24 cm with 30 watercolour pictures by John Wardle and 14 pages of clearly explained technical drawings. £11.99

Paperback books

A series of Peter's Railway in a smaller format. While the original books each contain several story or adventure threads, separate technical pages and Grandpa's tales, the small books concentrate on one aspect; an adventure, a tale from the old railways or a technical book. Age 6 - 12 years approx.

An adventure on a Scottish holiday ends with a bang!	A true story about an unlucky locomotive.	A dramatic true story from the old days.	A cab-ride in a modern train and a tale of disaster.	Our two heroes make a new engine from scrap.	Grandpa answers a tricky question.

"Little" Peter's Railway are gentle stories for younger children. Age 3 - 6 years approx.

The children foil a plot and cause destruction!

Peter saves Christmas, a gentle tale.

A bed-time story with a twist.

A railway picnic soon turns into mayhem...

SpringerBriefs in Philosophy

For further volumes:
http://www.springer.com/series/10082